CONE CAT

WRITTEN BY
SARAH HOWDEN

ILLUSTRATED BY
CARMEN MOK

OWLKIDS BOOKS

ONE DAY, Jeremy woke
up at the vet's,

and there was the Cone.

Like a giant white bell, it bent his whiskers,

  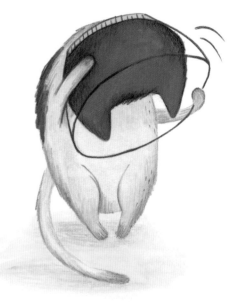

blocked his view,

and bungled his super cat senses.

I am Cone Cat now,
he told himself.

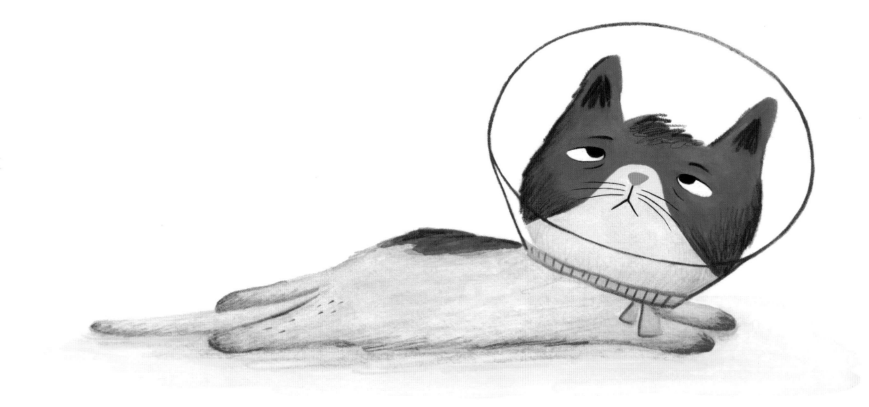

I will never be the same.

As Jeremy, he'd been nimble and quick.

And he'd prided himself on his sweet scent.

Now he was knocking into doorjambs and backing his way down the stairs with all the grace of a fat squirrel. He didn't smell so good either.

Clearly, the Cone was winning.

To take his mind off his problems, he tried to keep busy:

hunting,

redecorating,

and hiding from Ava,
the little human…

But nothing could shake his feline funk. Until a change landed
right in his lap. Well, his cone.

Ava had been eating breakfast as usual: Fruity O's and milk. His favorite. And as always, he'd jumped on the table to lap up the leftovers.

But this time, his tongue couldn't reach the bottom of the bowl.

Come on, Cone, he said. **Help me out!**

The Cone didn't answer.

Then something magical happened.
Just as Cone Cat wilted like the saddest flower...

the bowl tipped toward him.

Milk and cereal poured into his mouth—
and into the cone, too. He could save some for later!

Could the Cone be a
friend after all?

It got even
better.

That spider he
was stalking?

(It didn't taste as good
as he'd hoped.)

And the armchair unstuffing?
(Not a tuft left behind!)

Plus, if he directed the Cone just so, he could hear
Ava coming before she'd even left her room.

All of this led up to the greatest moment
of Cone Cat's life: Ava's birthday party.

Of course, a gathering of little humans can be a nightmare for a cat.

But then came the cake. And with it, ice cream.

Yes, the tall humans were serving ice cream in big, dollop-y scoops. Strawberry sprinkle surprise flavor.

The little humans all lined up with their bowls for the treat.

Cone Cat drooled, inching his way closer.

Was he seeing things, or did those bowls look familiar?

As the little humans spooned the stuff into their mouths like so much catnip, he pressed himself up to the front of the line and …

Before they could realize their mistake,
Cone Cat tiptoed off to a quiet place and
gobbled down the ice cream, licking up
every last drop.

It was heaven.

And it never would have happened
without the Cone.

The next day, Cone Cat felt one of the tall humans scritch-scratching his neck.

I hope they're not making you tighter,
he thought. Eh, Cone?

But suddenly,
it was off! His head
was free again!

Goodbye, he thought
as the human whisked
the Cone away.

Goodbye
forever.

Of course, he was
happy to be back to
his normal self,

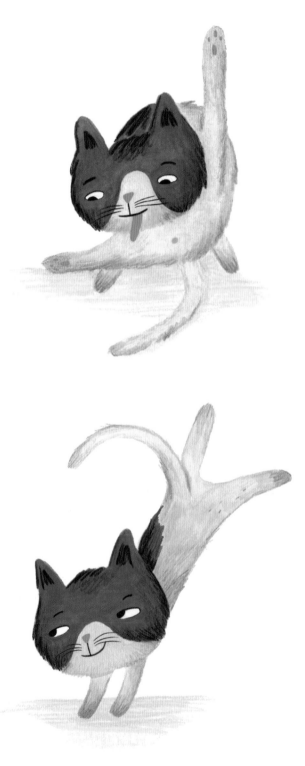

happy to be
Jeremy again.

ck, he wondered,

thing ever
to my glory
n the Cone?

It didn't take him
long to find out.

To Violet, the coolest (and cutest) cat I know — *S.H.*

To my forever best furry friends: Sasha and Max — *C.M.*

Text © 2020 Sarah Howden | Illustrations © 2020 Carmen Mok

Owlkids Books acknowledges the financial support of the Canada Council for the Arts, the Ontario Arts Council, the Government of Canada through the Canada Book Fund (CBF) and the Government of Ontario through the Ontario Creates Book Initiative for our publishing activities.

Published in Canada by Owlkids Books Inc., 1 Eglinton Avenue East, Toronto, ON M4P 3A1
Published in the US by Owlkids Books Inc., 1700 Fourth Street, Berkeley, CA 94710

Library of Congress Control Number: 2019955616

Library and Archives Canada Cataloguing in Publication

Title: Cone cat / written by Sarah Howden ; illustrated by Carmen Mok.
Names: Howden, Sarah, author. | Mok, Carmen, 1968- illustrator.
Identifiers: Canadiana 20190214465 | ISBN 9781771473613 (hardcover)
Classification: LCC PS8615.O935 C66 2020 | DDC jC813/.6—dc23

Edited by Karen Li | Designed by Alisa Baldwin

Manufactured in Guangdong Province, Dongguan City, China, in February 2020, by Toppan Leefung Packaging & Printing (Dongguan) Co. Ltd.   Job #BAYDC71

A   B   C   D   E   F

ONTARIO ARTS COUNCIL
CONSEIL DES ARTS DE L'ONTARIO
an Ontario government agency
un organisme du gouvernement de l'Ontario

Canada Council
for the Arts
Conseil des Arts
du Canada

Canada

Publisher of Chirp, Chickadee and OWL
www.owlkidsbooks.com   Owlkids Books is a division of    bayard canada